The Dinosaurs

ISBN 978-0-615-23582-0

The Dinosaurs

CHAPTER ONE

The name on the gold nameplate next to the door was Patrick Henry Adams, Senator from North Carolina. The place was the Hart Senatorial office building, Washington, D.C. Outside it was evening, traffic was zooming around the Capitol, the Politicians and Lobbyist were meeting in discreet paces to make deals. The meeting inside was the normal pre-election campaign briefing of Senator Adams and his loyal staff. They had been through five re-election campaigns. They were all sitting around the table in the conference room. At the head of the table was Senator Adams, he was now sixty seven years old, having been first elected in 1983 at the age of forty-two. He had solid white hair, deep lines ran across his forehead and his cheeks, which were now drooping jowls. He spoke in that senatorial speak, say a lot but say nothing. His weight had spread his stomach to a size fifty inches. He had to wear suspenders to keep his pants up. They were always bright red ones, it was his style, the old country boy look. He spoke in a low deeply southern voice that mumbled out of his mouth. Like Orson Wells in the movie, The Long Hot

The Dinosaurs

Summer. On his right was his top aid Jack Bennett. He has been with Pa Pa, as the all called him affectionately, for the whole twenty-five years he has been in office.   He was sixty years old with grey hair that was thinning on top. He was gaining a little more weight that comes with age but still not as big as Pa Pa He was also from North Carolina, raised on a Tobacco farm in the Piedmont. He had gone to the University of North Carolina and got his law degree. Pa Pa and him were from the same town, Stephen's Creek, they have known each other since boyhood. He always wore a suit no matter how hot it got. On Papa's left was Robert Dunn, fifty-nine years of age, still had most of his brown hair and was rail thin. He was the numbers cruncher for the team. On Jack's left was the newest addition to the group, Sam Gettis. Sam had joined the team in election of 1998. He was short, about five four, completely bald, still was young enough at forty to have the figure of a younger man. He ran most days, something Pa Pa couldn't understand. He was the "It" man. If something needed to get done or "Be taken of" he was the one to see it happened.

"How's it going, Boys?" asked Pa Pa

The Dinosaurs

"Looking good, still no one is running against you" answered Jack.

"Of course not, no one with any sense would run against me, I have my state sewed up, like a old spinster with her pocket book."

All at the table laughed out loud at this. No one has challenged Senator Adams for many years. He indeed had it sewed up.

"How's our money looking,Robert?" asked Pa Pa

" Already got the normal from the energy groups and the pill pushers. Still haven't heard from the Crusaders." answered Robert.

"Get on them, see if we can't stick them for more this time." said Pa Pa

The Crusaders was Papa's name for the Religious Right. He has been suckering them for years. They were so consumed with the far end of the religion scale and with the publicity the stance got them, you could get anything from them as long as you pretended to be on their side. Pa Pa always came up with a reason why a bill didn't get through. Mostly he blamed the Liberals. God bless the liberals. When you mentioned that word to the Crusaders they went blind with rage and forgot about you. Pa Pa often said,

"Nothing dumber than a Religious Fanatic"

"Keep on them". he continued.

"Anything else?"

"Next week we start of rounds of baby kissing and letting the home folks look at their great Senator." said Jack.

"God, I hate that, if only you could run without getting among the low life" said Pa Pa

"One good thing, next month we still are going to Puerto Rico" said Jack.

"Good, the Automobile lobby still funding that?" asked Pa-Pa

"They know you wouldn't miss that golf tournament."

"They should remember, after all we've done for them"

"That's just about it" stated Jack.

"Anything else, boys?" asked Pa-Pa looking at the rest around the table.

They all shook their heads no.

"That's it, see you at noon" said Pa-Pa.

He stood up and the rest followed him and they left the meeting room. Another hard day's work done.

Meanwhile, in the back room of a local gas station. This station was of the old kind. Pre-Modern. It was built of

The Dinosaurs

solid rock from the local area, had a mechanics bay or garage on one side and the storage room behind the front office that looked out a full window with a green metal awning that came halfway down the window. Most of the men of the town came by to sit, talk and maybe have a cold beer. It came out of one of those big ice chests or coolers from the fifties. You lifted up the top and reached in a got a beer or ice cold soft drink. On the side was still on of those beer bottle openers. In the back room there was a meeting going on. This wasn't any fancy meeting at the Capitol. It was in a little town at the footsteps of the Appalachian Mountains. It was called Newton. This is where men and women grew as hard and strong as the area around them. They had lived through every-thing that nature gave them. They have survived on the love of family and friends. They were people of the ground, the trees and love of God. Not the kind you see on TV, where thousands of people are led around by one man. They were led by local preachers, priests, rabbis and ministers of different faiths. They had been brought up believing it's not how much you give but what you did to help your fellow man. Now had come a time in this community

The Dinosaurs

where a decision was to be made that just might set off some fireworks. Inside the back room were the following men. Harry Bingham, the local barber. He was friendly, about fifty years old, lived here all his life. If he didn't know you, you were a stranger in town. He was about five six and one hundred and fifty pounds. Never a lost for words. Then came John Harrell, the banker, he was about five seven, had round metal frame glasses, wore a suit, but most of the times he carried the coat draped over his arm. He would have loosened the tie, but he had to maintain the look. Next was Jim Nixon the grocery store owner. He was five ten and little round in the middle,always had a good laugh, and as usual had on his white apron, a little soiled of course. Bryan Hughes was the gas station owner. He was five feet five inches tall with a big patch of red hair. He had on his overalls. His hands were washed but always appeared dirty and were rough from constantly using cleaning spirits. Finally was the Mayor, Pat Johnson. He had been mayor almost as long as Pa-Pa But he loved meeting the lower people as Pa-Pa put it. Across from them sat, Riley Nichols, he was a farmer, just getting by, in his mid fifties and was slim with black hair and deep brown eyes. He still had an athletic build from his days as a local high school star and working long hours in the fields. His eyes tended to look through you when talking to him or gleamed when he felt that something was humorous. He had the quiet that ran with his folks. The Cherokee Indians. He wasn't full blooded but had enough to make you want to raise your hand palm up and say

"How" when you met him.

"OK, guys, what's this about?" he asked.

First to speak was Mayor Johnson.

"Riley, we have all agreed that something needs to be done about our Senator, the Great Adams."

"I agree, but what can we do?" asked Riley.

"We need to run someone against him" said Jim.

"Who?" said Riley.

Harry, Jim, Pat, John and Bryan smiled at Riley.

"Oh, no. Not me" said Riley.

"It has to be you"

"You are the only one that can do it" repeated the mayor.

"I have no experience, no money, no Team"

The Dinosaurs

"We have already thought of that, we will supply the start off money and maybe some advice to boot." answered the Mayor.

Riley thought about this for a minute, why not. It would be hard to go up against Senator Adams and his machine. But he loved a challenge. And going along with his humor on things, he thought it just might be fun to see Senator Adams reaction. He had no chance of course, but maybe he could get people listening.

"OK, but you fellows have to be crazy, heck I have to be crazy too."

They sat there talking for a long while, planning and on how to start. Outside the clock turned to ten, the roads were empty and the traffic lights were blinking off and on. They reflecting on and off the front of the gas station. It was quiet and peaceful, well almost, somewhere out in the darkness a dog howled.

CHAPTER TWO

Any other town it wouldn't had made a stir. But in Newton it was a big to do. In Catawba County it was a big to do. Today was the first of the year and July 4th combined. The Committee to Elect Riley Nichols as U.S. Senator from North Carolina was standing on a flatbed trailer, it was about fourteen feet long, loaned from Pete Harris. Around the front was placed flag bunting. And at the back of the trailer was some small bales of hay. Standing there was Mayor Johnson, Harry Bingham, John Harrell. In the middle stood the sole object of all this attention. Riley Nichols. He was in his day to day clothes, short sleeve shirt and blue jeans with his work boots. As the Mayor came forward to say something the horn and drum section from the high school started up. It drowned out everybody. Finally when the Mayor thought he could jump in he raised his hands and started talking. The band director saw him and frantically motioned them to stop. They did, only not all at the same time.

"Ladies and gentlemen" said the Mayor

with arms outstretched.

He then cleared his voice, which caused the mike to squeal.

"That a boy, Mayor!" shouted a man in the back of the crowd.

The crowd laughed.

"We are here to announce that Riley Nichols is running for U.S. Senator from North Carolina and the great city of Newton."

The crowd went wild with excitement.

The Mayor raised his hands as if he was Moses parting the waters. The crowd went silent.

"It gives me great pleasure to tell you about Riley Nichols. He was born in this great county in 1951 in Newton Hospital. He was..."

"Come on Mayor, we know about Riley, let's hear from him" shouted the man in the rear again.

"OK, OK, it's my pleasure to introduce...." he was saying when the band started up again and drowned him out.

Riley came up to the mike and waved to the crowd. They burst into loud cheering and waving. Looking out over the sea of people, seeing his friends and neighbors, he wondered just what he was getting into. He raised his arms. The crowd fell silent, but the band was still playing. Soon the band director had their attention and all was quiet.

"All I can do is promise you that I will always be honest with you and most of all, listen to you. At anytime that I am Not, please kick me out. I know this is a long shot, with Senator Adams and his political machine, but with help from you and others we might just win." said Riley.

The crowd cheered. Back in the rear of the crowd there came a voice.

"You did good, Riley!"

The rest of the day was spent shaking hands and meeting people. He opened his campaign headquarters in Hughes Gas Station. He didn't have even any bumper stickers, he had a long ways to go.

The next day in Senator Adams office in Washington, Jack came in with a smile on his face.

"Looks like the cat has your tongue" said the Senator.

"Just got a call from the State Elections Board. It seems that some guy from Newton has decided to run against you."

"Newton, where the heck is that,

never heard of it." said the Senator.

"It's in Catawba County. Near the mountains." said Jack.

"What's his name?"

"Riley Nichols"

"Never heard of him, nothing to worry about" said the Senator.

But Riley took things serious.

He took some gas money from the campaign and started driving his old 1985 truck. It was grey and had some dents in it, but it ran good. He went to the store and got some of those writing books with the speckled front cover that they used when he was a student. He started going from home to home. It didn't matter if they were registered voters or not. He felt that all he people should be listened to. In the books he put their names, addresses and what bothered them and what help they wanted. Soon the word got around that someone was listening and actually taking notes. Soon people were waiting for him to come by. It was as if, you wasn't anybody till Riley came to see you. They all compared notes and those that were not registered when down to city hall and got signed up. The county was buzzing about the new man running for Senator.

The Dinosaurs

He then took his show on the road to neighboring counties. Soon same thing was happening here. The local snitches that Senator Adams had in the counties began to call up and complain about this new guy. There was too much talk about him and they were worried. They had been on the payroll of Senator Adams secretly for a long time and they didn't want to lose the money.

"Jack what is going on down there in Catawba County?" asked the Senator.

"Seems like this new fella is starting to stir up the locals" answered Jack.

"Call Sam" ordered the Senator.

Jack got on the phone and soon had Sam on the phone, he gave it to Pa-Pa.

"Sam, listen, go down to Catawba County and find all you can about this man Riley Nickels"

"Riley Nichols" corrected Jack.

"Riley Nichols" said the Senator.

"Find out what's going on and is he a threat to us, yea, thanks, Sam."

The Senator handed the phone back to Jack.

"I know he isn't a threat, but we can't let some upstart get going, can we?"

No Sir, never have let them before, besides Sam will take care of it." said Jack. The Senator quickly forgot the conversation. He never did worry about anyone running against him. They never made it, the Senator and Sam had their ways.

They knew the minute he got to town. He wasn't hard to spot. He drove a new Ford, like one of the police cars, and he had a sticker on the front windshield. It read, U.S. Senate, parking permit 094. He also wore a dark black suit. To say he didn't fit in was an understatement. Mr. Sam Gettis had arrived in Newton.

He didn't like being out of Washington, that was where he felt at home. He could wheel and deal there. Down here amongst the low life he felt uncomfortable. But he had a job to do, and he was very good at that job. All he had to do was gather the information and report back to Senator Adams. He didn't call him Pa-Pa like the others, he wasn't one of the old boys. He parked his car in front of Harry Bingham's Barber Shop. Through past experience he knew he could get local gossip there. He walked in and sat down in one of the chairs, there were two men sitting with him and one in the chair.

"Howdy" said Harry.

"Need a haircut?"

"No, I'm from the Raleigh Daily

The Dinosaurs

News, come here to see your man Riley Nichols" said Gettis with a straight face. Harry already knew who he was, the Newton Underground Information Line had already informed him.

"Yep, he is getting quite famous" said Harry.

"What can you tell me about him?" asked Gettis.

"Lived here all his life, a good man" said Harry.

"Has he held public office before, what are his qualifications?"

"No, never held no office"

"No qualifications I guess, just a Farmer"

"Is he married?" continued Gettis.

"Was, after he came back from the war, him and his wife spit up"

"War?"

"Yea, you know Viet Nam."

"They are still good friends, but sometimes people change." said Harry.

Mr. Gettis was busy taking notes in his little book.

This was too easy, thought Gettis, he was getting all the information that he needed here.

"There he goes" said Harry pointing to the sidewalk across the street.

Gettis turned around and got his

The Dinosaurs

first look at Riley Nichols. Wasn't very impressive he thought. A local with short shirt and blue jeans. On his head was a baseball cap with a red devil on it with NCHS underneath it. It was the Newton Conover High School mascot. What a bumpkin, he thought. But what caught his eye first was that this Riley Nichols was no white man.

"You say he is from here, doesn't look like anyone from around here?" said Gettis.

"Yea, some people do notice that, he's an Indian, Cherokee." answered Harry.

"Indian, I'll be" he said to himself.

"Thanks" he said to Harry as he left the barber shop to cross the street.

"Hi" said Gettis as he came up to Riley

"Hi" said Riley

"I'm from the Raleigh Daily News, I want to ask you a few questions."

"Sure, go ahead"

"What made you run for Senator?" asked Gettis.

"It was my neighbors and friends"

"What do you hope to accomplish?"

"To give the people a Senator that hasn't forgot about them and do my best to help them in any way I can" said Riley.

The Dinosaurs

Gettis went on the ask him more questions but he already had the information that he needed. He was just continuing the charade. Soon the interview was over, he got in his car and headed back to Washington.

The next day he reported to the old man.

"What did you find, Sam?" asked Senator.

Here's my report. Found out many things. If he gets too big for his britches we can smear him good.

Senator Adams took a few minutes to read the report.

"He's an Indian, a real Indian?" asked Senator Adams.

"Sure is" replied Sam

"You mean they are running an Indian against me?"

"He's a Cherokee." said Gettis.

"Heck, we have no problem, no one in North Carolina is going to vote an Indian into office of Senator of these United States."

"That's like voting a black into office, never happen" said the Senator.

"I thought this boy was a starting to be a threat"

"Nice job, I think we don't have to worry about this feller" said Adams.

CHAPTER THREE

Riley just keep doing what he thought was what he was supposed to do. He had never run as a Senator before, so he didn't know what was right and what was wrong. What he did was to continue to go door to door in his old pick up. Seeing the people one on one. He found out that not only must he visit them in the daytime but also at night. One such visit was with the Williamsons". They could hear his old truck squeaking and bouncing on the gravel driveway from the road to their house. Riley could swear he lost some teeth in that trip. The truck stopped and the door opened and shut and the dogs were barking. Riley had a trick for that, he always carried dog treats. He threw some at the dogs and behold they stopped barking. His dad always said,

"Son, a dog with a full mouth doesn't bite."

He always remembered that. Dan and Patricia Williamson came to the door and looked out. Dan recognized Riley and stepped out onto the porch. The house was like many houses in the south. It was Square with a kitchen and living room up front,two bedrooms and a bath. It had a wooden porch with skinny wood banisters and wood columns held up the porch. But like all poor Southern people they still had pride. They didn't have much but what they had by God it would be clean and neat. The driveway was lined with half buried car tires painted white. The mail box by the road was a cow that opened it's mouth when the box was opened. And at the foot of the front door was a mat that said it all.

"All Welcomed Here."

Riley went in and sat down in a chair in the living room, the Williamsons on the couch side by side. Dan was in his early sixties and Patricia was in her late fifties. The room had all the memories of family. There were rows of pictures sitting on end tables and other tables here and there. The TV was sitting on one of those food trays you used to sit and watch the TV. On top of the TV was a set of Rabbit Ears. Cable had not made it out here. If it was available, they could do without. They didn't ask for much. All they wanted was to live their life in peace. For their children to be well and happy. They would live out the rest of their lives here, content to sit on the porch and watch life go by.

The Dinosaurs

They told Riley about, Medicare Care and the cost of pills that the doctor prescribed for them. They told them about the cost of gas and the rising price of their food. Dan told him about the VA that was giving him a hard time about a benefit owed him. He told Riley about contacting Senator Adams but nothing ever seemed to get done. First all you got was an answering machine and if you finally got the office he was never in. Riley understood, he knew how the VA and the politics worked. First they never put someone in charge of the VA that really cared about the veterans. Always someone they owed a favor to. Riley listen almost two hours and took down pages of notes. He got up to say goodbye, when Mrs. Williamson got up walked over to him and hugged him. Riley didn't know what to do.

"I just want you to know you are the first person who actually came to see us and listen." she said with tears in her eyes.

"I might not be perfect Mrs. Williamson, but one thing my folks taught me. We are all here to help one another. And I will not forget you if I get into office, you can count of it." said Riley.

The Dinosaurs

Riley got into his pickup and started his engine and turned his lights on. The dogs came a running again. He threw out more treats. He waved good by, backed the truck up, turned around and headed down the driveway. In his rear view mirror he saw Dan and Patricia standing side by side on the porch holding each other around the waist waving to him. He will always remember that sight. These are the people that are the backbone of America. Common good people who just try to do the right thing in life and make it one day at a time. Never asking for much, but deserving much more. Riley had a bone in his throat thinking about them. And if he got elected by God he would not forget them.

Soon Riley was getting noticed by more than just the locals. He was becoming known across the state. A real reporter from the Raleigh Daily Times came by to see him. He sat down with Riley at his campaign office at the gas station. They both grabbed a soda from the cooler and sat down in chairs in the office. The reporter had his back to the window and Riley sat behind the desk that looked out upon the town and its people. It was his favorite place, to sit here and watch the them go. He always got a good feeling from that. By watching he felt all was good in Newton and all was right in the world. Since he was a boy if he had a table or desk in front of him, he just naturally stretched out his legs and put his feet up on top. He did it without thinking. His mom had always corrected him, but he still had the habit.

"Seems like you are starting to make a stir in this Senatorial campaign, Mr. Nichols" said the reporter.

"Just call me Riley"

"I'm just trying to give the people the representative they need."

"Explain that"

"The men, like Senator Adams, have been there so long they're becoming arrogant. They actually think they know what's better for the people than the people. They don't listen to them anymore. They are brought out to the lobbyist. They have become millionaires. They think they have done a good job. But you must think what the country is like now. Messed up. And who was there during all this time, making all these decisions. The Dinosaurs of course."

"The dinosaurs?" asked the reporter.

"I call them the Dinosaurs, the Old Senators who have been there forever. They will never change. Every election

they come out, promise the same things.
They don't change any ethics panels.
They have lived passed their time. It's
time for new blood, maybe not me, but
the changing of he guard is needed. Time
to put the Dinosaurs out to pasture."
        "I never heard it put that way"
        "Some of it is your fault." said Riley.
        "My fault?"
        "Yes, your paper and others never
report on how they voted, never ask them
questions, you never hear from them.
Out of sight out of mind."
        "That's true, my paper have never,
since I've been here had a good in depth
interview with the Senator."
        "The dinosaurs depend on the
people being complacent. That as long as
it doesn't bother me, I don't care attitude.
But the times they are a changing. The
baby boomers from the sixties that rallied
against the war are now starting to rally
against the dinosaurs. Yep, change she is
a coming."
        "Do you think you can actually
win?"
        "I'm no idiot, I know what kind of
political machine I'm up against. I know
it will get dirty, I know how they fight.
Who knows, maybe the stars are aligned
this time" Riley said as he smiled.

The Dinosaurs

"I will be covering you, you will see me more and more, you are the hot news now. They talked some more. The morning grew on, the reporter found himself not wanting to leave. There was something about this Nichols that he liked. Maybe it was he was easy to talk too, he listened, really listened to what you had to say. And there was a wisdom about him. The reporter thought, he might just make this a race. Even though he wasn't supposed to, he found himself pulling for him.

He was hot alright. That week CNN came down to Newton and did a story on him. Soon other networks came. He started showing up in newspapers. His campaign started raising more money. All this attention came to the office of Senator Adams.

"Jack, it's time to fight back, this Nichols is getting too much attention, get Sam in here" ordered Pa Pa

The Senator was sitting behind his desk, Jack and Sam were sitting in chairs in front facing him.

"Sam, start the ball rolling, phase one of smear Nichols"

"Yes Sir." answered Sam

"Now is the time to get him, before the idiot people get behind him" said Pa

The Dinosaurs

Pa

"Jack, you with this?"

"Of course, Pa Pa, nothing new, we have done it before, a slam dunk." he said.

"Good, time to call in the head Crusaders"

With that the ball started rolling.

The Dinosaurs

CHAPTER FOUR

Later that week, sitting in Senator Adam's office was the Head Crusaders. There was Rev. Caldwell. He had a university he named Freedom. He even had a law school that put out his opinions and did his bidding. He had a lot of influence with the Religious Right. He had them from birth to death. All he had to do was put the fear of God in them and the fear of death. People, when they got older, always got serious about God and death. And he knew how to tweak that fear. They were like lambs led to the slaughter. Just follow the leader, no matter if he was leading them to hell.

Also in his office was Rev. Donaldson. He had a TV program that appeared twice daily around the country. He also had a great influence with the Religious Right. Sometimes he went too far in saying and predicting things, but the sheep that followed him never swayed away.

"Glad you both could make it" said the Senator.

"Anytime" said Rev. Caldwell

"Same here" said Rev. Donaldson

"We have a problem, and I me we."

said the Senator.

"What is it, Pa Pa" asked the Rev. Caldwell.

"Yes, what?" asked Donaldson

"There is a man running against me, and if he gets elected he will create problems for both me and you."

"You mean Riley Nichols?" asked Rev. Caldwell.

"I see that you have heard of him" said the Senator.

"Who hasn't, he's on all the morning talk shows" said Rev. Caldwell

Here's the problem. If he's elected, he won't back you like me. He won't push
your agenda and put Conservatives on the court."

Both Reverends looked at each other.

"Also he is an Indian. Now we all know that the white conservative is the man God wanted to run his show. We are supposed to minister to the Indians, Blacks and others below the white man, you know that." said the Senator.

"This is true, all through the ages it's been the white man who has discovered new places and ministered to the heathens." said Rev. Donaldson.

"I need your help." asked the

Senator."

"What do you need" said both.

"I want you to start preaching to your flocks about what will happen to the state if an Indian is elected, after all he is a heathen."

"Also, I need to raise some money to fight him"

"We will have a emergency fund raising, to stop the liberals from getting into office and the normal liberal stuff we give them." said Rev. Caldwell.

"Works every time." said Rev. Donaldson.

"Good, you know how to funnel it into my cash account."

"Thanks for your help." said the Senator as they got up to leave.

"With God's help we'll fight these Liberal and anti-Christians." said the Senator.

"Amen" both the Reverends said.

The very next day, both Christian Networks had a emergency fund raising to fight the Anti-Christian groups trying to get into the government. And it worked, the fear of God. They were raising money hands over fists. Works every time.

Then the campaign videos started coming out. They didn't come out and say.

"Don't vote for Riley,"
because he was an Indian. They did it
very professionally. More like,

"Would you want a man like this to
represent your state?"

While showing a Indian in tattered
clothes and drinking whiskey. They had
experience at this, they had done this
before.

The phone rang.

"Senator, it's Mr. Smith for you."
said his secretary Debbie. She has been
with the Senator for the last fifteen years.

"Ok, Debbie, put him on two." said
the Senator.

"Hello Ben, how's it going? Sorry to
hear that, the IRS, huh. Don't worry
about it, I give them a call." the Senator
hung up.

"Debbie, call Pete at the IRS for me.
Let me know when you have him."

A few minutes later Debbie said,

"On line three, Senator"

"Thanks Debbie"

"Hey Pete, how's the family, did they
enjoy the vacation in Bahamas?"

"Good, look I have a friend that's
having a little problem. It seems like you
want to audit his company. He told him
the name of the corporation, yea I know

about the rumors. Give me some love here, Pete."

"Great, I'll tell him. Look how about Ireland this year."

"No problem, after all what are friends for."

"Keep in touch Pete, again thanks" with that the Senator had done a big favor for a friend who happened to be a big donor.

"Debbie, get me Ben again."

"Hey, no problem, no audit. Anytime. Remember election is coming up soon. Oh, that's too much. I know you appreciate it. Do it anytime. Again, thanks for the contribution." The Senator hung up. It had been a very fruitful morning. He got an extra one hundred thousand dollars for his campaign.

Back at the campaign office sat Riley and the reporter.

"What's up Tom?" asked Riley

Since they were going to be close together, Riley finally got to know his name, Tom Peters.

"The big man in Washington has started his campaign against you and it's getting dirty" said Tom

"I knew it would"

"There's more, my boss got a call

from the Senator and he put the squeeze on him. Reminding him about a bill he could introduce to limit the size of local Newspapers"

"Would he go that far?"

"My boss thinks so"

"He's been told by the Senator to start printing anything negative he can find on you"

"So much for freedom of the press" said Riley.

"What are you going to do?" asked Tom

"Nothing now, just keep visiting the people of North Carolina."

"Be careful, remember Kerry did that and look what happened to him." said Tom.

"Don't worry, when the time comes, he will hear from me." smiled Riley. Riley was right, he just kept visiting the people, listening to them and taking notes down in his books. And his popularity kept growing, much to the disdain of Senator Adams. The Smear Videos didn't seem to have worked as they did in the past. Next on to stage two.

Back in the office of Senator Adams it was getting hot.

"I don't get it" said the Senator.

The Dinosaurs

"It doesn't seem to be working"

"I don't understand it either" said Jack

"Next step, go for his military time, let's Swift Boat him" ordered the Senator.

"Will do" said Jack.

The commercials came out that week. They were saying that Riley hadn't really earned his medals that he was in the rear during the war. They even had some men from his platoon say that. Of course, what they didn't say was that these men were members of the Christian Right and followed their orders like good Crusaders.

Of course the Right Sighted newspapers picked up on this. And the Far Right cable news shows sent reporters to Newton to find out why Riley was lying about his military time.

They were all packed into the little office with notepads, mikes and cameras. Riley just sat back in his chair with his Red Devils hat on and smiled.

"They all started asking questions at once."

Riley held up his hands and said,

"Gentleman, one at a time, I will try to answer all your questions, want a cold soda?"

"Yea, I'll take one" said one of the

reporters.

The first one to ask a question was from Murdoch Stations. A far right news organization.

"Mr. Nichols, why have you lied about you time in Viet Nam?"

"I never lied, I was in Viet Nam" smiled Riley.

"No, I mean your time in the Infantry"

"I never lied, I was in the Infantry, from 1969 to 1970."

"How come you claim to have gotten medals for things you did not do?"

"I never claimed that I never got medals for things I never claimed I didn't do."

"The Christian Right has men from your platoon saying you didn't do anything to earn them."

"From my platoon? You don't have their names do you? I would like to get in touch with them." said Riley.

"What do you say to the fact that they said you didn't earn them?" asked the reporter.

"Everyone has an opinion and you know what they say about opinions"

The reporter looked at him, puzzled, of course he didn't know what they said.

Tom Peters did, he sat in the corner

and smiled. He watched a boy from the hicks handle these big time reporters like a professional. At the end of the day, they were so confused that they actually thought they had gotten the story.

It seems that the world and the people of North Carolina got it. A huge chuckle went out over the airwaves. All the late night comedians were telling jokes about it. Only one place didn't like the jokes.

The room was getting hotter. Senator Adams was starting to get mad.

"What's wrong with the world, it always worked before." said the Senator.

"Don't get it, just don't get it" said Jack.

"It's got to work, keep the military thing going, this time focus on his coming back and splitting up with his wife. Do the mental thing, came back crazy."

"Ok, boss" replied Jack.

They finally found her, the ex Mrs. Nichols. Sarah was working in her shop on Green Street. She had on an apron with flowers on it. She ran the The Not So Green Thumb Garden Shop. She was five feet seven inches tall, average weight with brown hair with grey streaks in it. She had green eyes that twinkled when she smiled. She was standing out front watering some hanging plants when the mob descended on her. She turned around and jumped a little when they approached.

"Mrs. Nichols, Mrs. Nichols," they all yelled at one time.

"Whoa! There honey, you just slow down, take your time and then ask." she said as if she was talking to a young child. The reporter took a deep breath and continued.

"Mrs. Nichols, is it true you and your husband divorced because of Viet Nam?"

"Why no honey, who told you that?"

"Is it true that your husband came back scarred from the war?"

"Sure it is, honey, it's on his left back shoulder, about three inches long."

"So you are admitting he was scarred from the war."

"Sure honey." she repeated.

"You admit he wasn't right when he came back from the war."

"Heck honey, he wasn't right when he left for the war."

"You admit he came back crazier than when he left?"

"Oh no, honey, he was pretty crazy when he left."

"How do you mean?" he asked.

The Dinosaurs

"Well, honey, he married me, didn't he." she burst out laughing with that twinkle in her eye. Off the side was Tom Peters. He was smiling, yep, he thought, no wonder Riley and her got along. Still smiling he turned around and left, he had seen this show before, he knew how it would turn out. So did the late night shows. Riley and his wife, Sarah were putting on a hit show. The interview was showed everywhere.

Later in the week the reporters were back again. They were all trying to get the first question in. There were four men reporters and one women. All of them blurted out a question at the same time. The women's voice was drowned out by the men.

"Honey, honey, wait a minute. Don't you see this young lady with you?"

"That's no lady, that's a reporter." said one male.

They all laughed, including the women.

"Well, let me tell you how Miss Sarah works. Anytime there's a lady with you, she gets the first question." She gave them "The Stare". She got it from her mother. She would give you that look and you knew you were in trouble. The male reporters all answered.

The Dinosaurs

"Yes ma'am"

"There you go, that wasn't hard, was it."

"Come on in, it's getting hot out here, I have some of my special Kool Aid ready."

They all went in and had a very different type of interview. She was honest, open and soon they found themselves falling into her loving personality. Of course the lady got the first question.

CHAPTER FIVE

Senator Adams was sitting at his desk the next day when a fellow Southern Senator came in.

"Hello, Patrick, taking it easy?" he asked

"Getting ready to do the grind, go out and see the retards back home." he said.

The other Senator laughed.

"Yea, me too. You shouldn't have any problem this year, just like all the rest."

"Not really, this year I have a recreant running against me this time."

"Oh yea, the Indian."

"You've heard." said Senator Adams

"Don't worry, no one will vote the Indian into office."

"Good luck" said the Senator as he left the office.

"You're darn right he won't make it to office." said Senator Adams to himself.

Riley was down on North Roxboro Street in Durham. Not the most upper class or rich section of Durham. He chose this area to give a campaign speech just for that reason. No one ever came down here to give a campaign speech.

The Dinosaurs

At first only a few came up to the truck, people thought he was a farmer selling vegetables. Then the word got out that Riley was in town and in their neighboyhood.

"Howdy folks" said Riley with a smile.

The folks immediately took to him. There was something about the way he looked at you, the way he talked. There was an honesty to his voice, you knew he was one of them, he had walked the dog and come on home.

"Howdy, glad you came. I guess you know who I am. I am running for the seat of Senator Adams."

"Booo.oooo!" went the crowd.

"I take it he isn't your favorite Senator."

The crowd laughed and Riley laughed with them.

"I'm going to give a little speech, but I'm not leaving. The County won't let me into the school here, so when it gets a little cooler I'm going to set up a chair behind my truck over there in the shade and listen to every one of you that wants to talk." The crowd was stunned. Stay and talk, that's something new. But that's how Riley did business. No matter how long it took he would stay and listen to the people.

Over in Raleigh, at the Country Club, Senator Adams was giving his normal re-election speech. He was dressed in a fine suit. At the tables sat the upward crust of the society, dressed in their finest. On the tables were Caviar and expensive wine. After all it was a thousand dollar a plate dinner.

"I need your help this year. I have a opponent running against me. You and me can't let him win. All we have done in the past twenty years will go up in smoke. He will turn this state back over to the uneducated and turn it back into a society of people who can't get up and get a job."

"We have worked to hard to make this state that believes in God and his will to have us guide its people."

"So in the name of God join the fight with me, turn back these heathens, Join the Fight!"

He yelled with his arms waving in the air. The crowd jumped up out of their seats yelling, "Fight the Heathens! Fight for God!"

The Senator looked out at the crowd. I got them hooked he thought, working for God works every time. He smiled out at them.

The Dinosaurs

It was getting late, the street lights had come on. The police had rode by several times. Thinking no good was going on, after all this was North Roxboro Street. The crown had gone, he was tired, it had been a long day. While he was putting his folding chair back on the truck and the books inside the cab an old black lady came up to him.

"May I talk to you a minute, Mr. Nichols"

"Sure can, ma'am" he answered.

He got the chair out. He opened it, but instead of sitting in it himself he asked to old lady to sit. His mother had raised him right. He sat down with his legs crossed and folded underneath him.

"What can I do for you... wait a minute ma'am"

He got up, went to the cab and got one of his books.

He again sat down again with his legs folded under him.

"Sorry, ma'am, forgot my book."

She smiled.

"Now what can I do for you?" he continued.

For the next forty five minutes he listened to her. He didn't know it but he was being watched. In the houses along the street and on porches there were eyes watching him. One by one they slowly shook their heads in an affirmative manner. They were approving of this Riley fellow. They watched him take his time with Old Molly. He was kind and gentle with her. When she was through he walked her to her house and held the door open for her. She smiled. In the school parking lot he got into his truck and headed out for another spot tomorrow.

Back at the Country Club the Senator was winding up his speech. His speech had worked, he got twice the money he had gotten last election time. As soon as he finished he was ready to leave. Going out the door a old lady stopped him.

"Senator, Senator, wait I need to talk to you about my Social Security"

The Senator turned around.

"Sorry, I have to leave now, I have another speaking engagement." he said.

"But..."

"Here's my card, write to me and I will get my clerks right on it" he said as he was leaving.

"God these people drive me nuts" the Senator muttered under his breath.

The old lady took the card, looked at it, put it in her pocketbook and went

The Dinosaurs

back to her friends. To tell them that the
Senator will personally help her. She was
proud that she knew the Senator so well.

CHAPTER SIX

Senator Adams was stretched out on his couch in his bus. It had everything, bed, Television, bathroom and shower. Even a stove and refrigerator. Him and Jack were watching the local television station. WRMD in Raleigh. On it was news anchor Bob Rayburn. He was giving the latest political roundup.

"Good evening, it's seems there might be a race for U.S. Senator after all." he started.

"The double digit lead that Senator Adams had at the beginning of this political season is gone." he continued. The Senator raised up off the back of the couch and leaned forward to listen.

"The polls list Senator Adams at fifty four per cent and the newcomer Riley Nichols at forty five per cent. Senator Adams has a lead of just nine per cent.

"What!" Senator Adams screamed.

"Don't fret, Pa Pa" they go either way at plus or minus four per cent." said Jack.

"Don't fret, that means it could be a difference of only five per cent."

The news anchor continued.

"It seems everyone is wondering,

when will there be a debate"

"Debate, why I haven't debated anyone in years." said the Senator as it was unimaginable.

"Jack, call the operatives in the counties, get out the poll machine."

"Like we did last election?" asked Jack.

"The same." he answered.

Jack got on the phone in the bus and called all the operatives. What the operatives were to do is volunteer on line for Polls. The poll people were always looking for new blood. They would sign up as different parties, different ages and of course stack the polls in his favor. It worked last time when he was behind. The people watched his polling numbers go up and in the end he gained more votes. There is always a way to rig the results.

"Senator, can I have a minute with you?" asked Debbie.

"Sure, you know you can anytime, Debbie." answered the Senator.

"You see, it's my son, he was arrested last night."

"What for Debbie?" asked the Senator.

"It seems he was at this party with a friend when it was busted by the DEA.

The Dinosaurs

He was just there, Senator, my son doesn't do drugs"

"Can you help him?"

"Well, Debbie, the DEA is serious business. I can't go jumping into a DEA investigation. You know it's election time, I can't afford to be seen giving out favors. You understand, don't you. Good, now back to work."

Debbie had never asked the Senator for help before and this time he just shook her off. She had seen him help others, she wondered why not her, she had been a faithful employee for over fifteen years.

The debate was on. It was sponsored by WRMD and the narrator was Bob Rayburn. It was to be in two weeks at the RBC Center in Raleigh. Senator Adams wasn't worried. He had always won debates. He was just too good and experienced at it. He was confident.

Riley was nervous, he had never been in front of that many people before. He was used to small crowds, one on one communication. Tom Peters went over earned from debates he had covered in the past. The man thing he stressed was just be yourself, if you don't know a answer to a question, don't make one up.

The Dinosaurs

Be honest and truthful.

He was nervous because the polls had changed in the last two weeks. The Senator had gone back to double digits. He was wondering if he had reached his top. Was the dream over.

The night was here. Sarah had come to his side. Like she did so many times before. They had a deep love for each other, but when he came back from the Nam, he had changed. It tore their marriage apart. He had sought help and learned some things were just out of his control. He had talked to other veterans and found out it was alright for him to feel the things that he was feeling. And Sarah was always there. Always by his side, always beside him in the dark lonely night when he would call to her for help. She held him in the dark while he cried and let out all the bad things that the Nam had left in him. They had come through the pain, the forgiveness, and the healing together. She never said no, never turned away. He loved her deeply. She was here tonight, in the front row seat. He knew that whenever he needed her she would be there. Always.

Riley came out on the sage first. He was dressed in a dark blue suit loaned to him from The Green Room, a local

The Dinosaurs

Community Theater group in Newton. It
was one that Paul Newman wore in the
movie, From the Terrace, or just like it. It
fit him well.   He was standing there for a
few minutes when the Senator came
out. He looked like a Senator. White
hair, with his suit coat opened and those
red suspenders showing. He had learned
that trick a long time ago. It made the
audience wait and when you finally came
out, all attention was on you. Poor
Riley Nichols, he thought, he didn't have
a chance. The Old Pro was in the house.
He chuckled to himself. Riley looked out
at the sea of faces. He took a hard
swallow, almost lost it for a moment. He
looked down and he saw Sarah. She
smiled that crazy smile at him and waved
to him, giggling. Instantly he relaxed.
Good ole Sarah, never changes. The
reporters and the people noticed it too.
Over the months they had fallen in love
with her. Who wouldn't have.

The narrator began. The crowd went
silent.

"I'm going to ask you a question. I
will give both of you two minutes to
answer. I will alternate between you for
the first answer."

Both men were behind a podium
standing up. It began.

The Dinosaurs

"What should be do about the War in Iraq?" he asked.

"Senator, you first."

"We can't leave, it would create such a mess. The area would turn into a hot bed for terrorists. We have such an opportunity for a freely elected govern-ment. It will take patience, more money, and more sacrifice from our hero troops. Remember, we have to fight them there and not over here."

"Mr. Nichols?"

"It always amazes me that people who have never been to war, are always the first to yell, we must sacrifice. War destroys families. Only Moms and Dads, Grandmothers and Granddads, Sisters and Brothers know how it feels to lose a loved one. More sacrifice? No bring them home now. Save them now. Bring them home. Let's have no more broken hearts in America."

"That's just like you Liberals. Crying over spilled milk. You die in war. You have to make sacrifices. It's just the way war is." said the Senator.

"Senator, you must refrain from speaking out of turn." said the narrator.

"Mr. Nichols would you like to answer that?"

"I only have one question for the

The Dinosaurs

Senator. What sacrifices have you made?"

"A lot, you upstart."

"Alright, next question" said the narrator.

"What would you do about the listening to peoples conversation via phones, mail and or e-mail."

"Mr. Nichols?"

" I would investigate what has been happening against the law. I would make the President come out with the truth. I would make sure that the party in the executive branch understood that you have to have a court order first.

"Senator?"

"There you go again, always talking about our rights. This is a different place and time. Not two hundred years ago. We don't have time to make sure that peoples rights are not violated. We have to get the information now. Remember we have to fight the terrorists over there not here."

"What do you think about global warming?"

"Senator?"

"Here we go again. More hogwash put out by the Liberals. There is no global warming. Our scientists have proven it. The earth gets warmer and colder all the time. We just happen to be in a warming cycle." he smiled.

"Mr. Nichols?"

"Yes, we are in a warming cycle. But it isn't natural. It's brought on by corporations who are more interest in the bottom line, profit, than the earth and it's future. We must enforce the EPA laws that are on the books, not make new ones. Also think about this. Trees make oxygen, we have cut down Old Forests in South America, Indonesia and elsewhere including forest in America. If one out of ten people planted new trees this year, don't you think it will make a difference in twenty years. Think about it."

The crowd clapped. From the back of the auditorium came a familiar voice.

"That's the way to tell'em."

The crowd laughed again.

"I must remind you in the audience you must re frame from yelling out." said Bob Rayburn.

It was quieting down when you heard that infectious laugh of Sarah. The crowd heard it, and they couldn't help it, they broke out again. The narrator stifled a giggle too.

"The next question. What do you think about all this controversy about secret earmarks?"

"Senator"

The Dinosaurs

"Well you have to keep them secret. If the people knew before hand what you were earmarking, some would feel left out, they would all be calling and before you knew it, the office would be to busy with answering phones calls than working on earmarks. You understand, it's just the way business has been done in Washington."

"Mr. Nichols?"

"Yes it's true that is the way business has always been done in Washington. All in secret. Instead of having a few, those usually that contribute a lot to campaign chests. And to corporations that contribute to campaign chest and only going to areas that are well populated and have heavy voter turnout for the Senator. Why not try this approach. That these millions of dollars that are handed out each year, say, give one million to the poorest county to build a school. And the next year give it out to another poor county for schools. Or even for a medical center that they have needed for a long time. You can make it two or three or four counties each year that never get any Earmarks. Everyone would know that their turn was coming, they wouldn't be left out. It would be fair and open and above board."

The Dinosaurs

"Poppy Cock! It would never work!"
said the Senator out loud.

"Senator, you must re frame from
your Comments"

The debate went on for about an hour.
The narrator asked the last question.

"Gentlemen, I will give each of you
fifteen minutes to make a last statement.
Before we stated we flipped a coin to
see who would go first."

"Senator, you first."

The Senator thought everything had
gone his way, even the coin toss. He
began.

"Ladies and Gentlemen, I have been
your Senator from North Carolina for over
twenty years. I have been honored to
represent you. I have always done what is
good for you. I know, sometimes, it
seems I haven't listened to you but let me
explain the system. I know the system, I
am on very powerful committees. I have
been there so long I really don't need to
ask you, I know automatically what is
good for you. It might not seem so at the
time, but trust me, it was always for your
good. I will be proud to represent you for
another six years. Don't take the chance
of losing powerful committee seats to a
newcomer, who wouldn't know how to
piss in a pot. Excuse me, that's just my

down home talk. Please elect me again, thank you"

With that he opened his coat jacket and showed the audience his down home boy suspenders.

"Mr. Nichols"

"Well, it's true I don't have all those committees. The good Senator says he knows the system. I just bet he does. It's made him very rich. I want you to answer one question. When was the last time the Senator came to your county, your community? I know he comes to the heavy populated ones, where there are a lot of voters. When was the last time he went to all the counties, big and small. A long time, if ever. When was the last time he actually sat down for more than it takes to flash a camera, say a few words and then leave. Even worse, the Senator comes back to North Carolina and he disappears. You don't see him, the television and radio stations act like we don't have a Senator, you never hear of how he voted, they never cover it. Or why he voted for or against a bill. They just don't report about him. Why? He just disappears off the radar. But come election time he's everywhere an buddies with everyone. How man times are you going to fall for this, how many? He's

The Dinosaurs

depending that you never catch on. All I
can promise you it that I will always
listen to you. I will always do my best for
you. I will make mistakes, all people do. I
will ask for your guidance. After all, it
was people like you that made this state
and this country great. It's time to kick
out all the Dinosaurs. (The crowd and
reporters picked up on that phrase, in
was in all the newspapers the next day)
All I ask it that you give me a chance.
Thank You. Goodnight."

    The auditorium broke into clapping.
    "That liberal boohoos!"
    "They will never vote for you, I own
them, they are mine."
    "Senator, Senator, the mike is still
on." said the narrator.
    Finally it was over. The Senator
went down to the end of the stage and
was getting ready to shake hands and
meet the reporters. When he got to the
first row seats, he found out that he was
alone. All the people and reporters had
headed to the other side to see Riley.
    "What's going on here, Jack?" asked
Senator Adams.
    "He's just the new boy in town, Pa
Pa, don't worry, you still have it sewed
up."
    They both left by the rear door, got

into their bus and headed back to Washington. Pa Pa always felt more at home there. It had been a long time since he felt that way about North Carolina.

"How do you feel?" asked Tom Price to Riley.

"Feels like I'm been through a hay grinder." said Riley.

"Yea, but you did good tonight, real good." said Tom.

Standing by the front row, Sarah was taking pictures of all the ruckus. Many women and some reporters were trying to get interviews with her. The Senator had left in his bus not even stopping for the parking lot attendant. After all he was a Senator, perks came with that.

Riley couldn't wait to get out of that suit. His truck was waiting for him in the back parking lot. He didn't know how much he would have to pay for that parking ticket. Riley pulled up to the building where the parking lot attendant was at. He took out the ticket and handed it to him.

"Evening Sir, Heard it on the Radio. You were great." said the Attendant.

"Thank You, I was scared to death."

"I just want you to know I will vote

for you."

"Thanks, how much?"

"Ten dollars, Sir, but you don't have to, Senator Adams didn't so I guess you don't have too either."

"No, you work hard at your job, and this helps pay for that."

"Here's the ten, and a dollar to boot." said Riley.

"Geez" said the young attendant.

"See Ya Dude" said Riley as he waved to the attendant.

CHAPTER SEVEN

Riley and Tom were sitting in the old campaign headquarters in Newton. Tom with his legs stretched out in front of him. Riley leaned back in the chair behind the desk with his legs stretched out on the desk. Tom was looking at Riley, he was a little thinner, the skin under his eyes were a little darker.

"Riley, you're looking tired, I think you should take a break from this campaigning for a while."

"After all, you are now dead even with the Senator in the polls."

"Yea, I am tired, maybe I'll go up to the City Lake and fish for a while."

"I'll hold down the fort, go take a break, you need it."

"Thanks, Tom" said Riley adjusting the Red Devils hat on his head. They sat there drinking their cold soda's, not talking, just taking in another quiet cool morning in Newton. Meanwhile, back in the Washington, Senator Adams was on the phone talking to newspaper mogul Ruford Murdoch

"Hello, Ruford, how are you doing?"

"Good, good, fine, doing fine. Look I need your help in something."

The Dinosaurs

"Look we need to dig something up on this Riley Nichols fellow, they say he's even with me in the latest polls. Thanks, anytime I can help you, you just call, you know you can depend on it."

He hung up the phone knowing that Murdoch would dig up the dirt or if he couldn't, he would make it up. He thought,

"That's what makes America great."

A few days later Sarah was outside talking to her best friend, Ida. They had known each other since childhood.

It was still in the morning the sun was shining, but not hot, on their backs. Sarah was facing the sun which was behind Ida. She held her hand over her eyes to block the sun rays.

" You still going to the Movie in the Park Thursday."

"Of course, they are showing Happy Feet in Southside Park, you coming?"

"Sure, I'll meet you there at seven, in time to see the band before the movie." she answered.

"Oh, Oh, Sarah, looks like some out of town people heading your way."

Sarah turned to look where Ida was looking and she saw them. A women with long blond hair, and two men. One with a notebook and the other with a camera.

"Just some more news people, I swear I don't see what they see in me, it's Riley that's running." Ida had to jump out of the way when they reached them on the sidewalk. The women almost bumped her off the sidewalk.

"Hey!, just ask, I'll move" said Ida.

"Mrs. Nichols" the women started.

"Just call me Sarah" Sarah said.

"I prefer not too" answered the reporter.

"What can I..." asked Sarah.

The reporter didn't let her get the question out.

"I want to ask you about the death of your son."

Sarah was stunned, she had not talked about that for a long time, it brought up to many sad memories.

"I understand that it was your fault that he died, isn't that right?"

"You shouldn't talk to Sarah like that..." said Ida.

Before she could finish the reporter broke in.

"Listen lady, I don't know who you are, but stay out of this, it's none of your business."

"My name is Le Ann Bolton, and I am a member of the media. I have every right to be here and get the story."

"I have you know that Sarah is my friend and....."

"Bill!" said the reporter to one of her male companions.

Bill stepped in front of Ida and began pushing her aside.

"Go lady, get!" he shouted.

Ida almost fell over with the shove. She left running down the street.

"Listen lady, we know he wasn't supposed to be driving that night, he only had a learner license."

"But he only went down to the corner store, he had done it before." said Sarah.

"So you admit you broke the law and let your son drive that night." said Le Ann.

"Well, no,..."

Again before she could answer.

"You did let him go and he had no license." she shouted.

Le Ann turned to the camera and said,

"You see she is trying to hide the fact that she is guilty."

"What else is she trying to hide?:

"Isn't it true that he was speeding and ran off the road and hit a tree. Isn't it?"

The Dinosaurs

"He ran off the road, I don't know if he was speeding..."

"You don't know, I know why you don't know. It took you a hour before you checked on him, isn't that true?" grinned Le Ann.

She knew she had her now. Sarah was backing up, but the outside flower pots stopped her movement. She was caught between them and the reporter. The lights of the camera were in her face.

"He always stopped to talk to his friends that were hanging out at the store." answered Sarah.

"Isn't it true it took you over an hour to look for your son?"

"You're denying the officers report?" asked Le Ann quickly before Sarah could answer.

"No..ooo." answered Sarah.

Again, Le Ann looked into the camera and stated,

"Viewers at home why is she lying to me and to you about the time. Why?" she smiled into the camera.

"I didn't know that he had an accident. I didn't know" said Sarah low and sadly to herself.

"Riley! Riley! Yelled Ida as she ran into the Barber Shop. She grabbed the desk to get her breath back. Tom

Price and Riley jumped up and guided her to the couch. She sat down.

"What's got you so excited, Ida?" asked Riley.

"It's Sarah, she need's help."

Riley jumped to attention and asked,

"What's wrong with Sarah?"

"There are three reporters who are asking her about Stephen."

"Oh no."

"Where is she, Ida?"

"She's in front of her store, go help her."

Riley ran out of the Gas Station as fast as he could run, with Tom a little behind him. When he was approaching the shop he saw that Sarah was pinned against the front with the reporter hounding her. She looked scared. Nothing more can get Riley's blood up than someone mistreating Sarah. He jumped in between Sarah and the blond reporter.

"What's going on here?" asked Riley.

"Well, look whose here, the candidate himself."

"No more questions about our son, this interview is over." said Riley.

Le Ann looked into the camera and said,

The Dinosaurs

"See folks, what are they hiding and why don't they want you to hear it."

"I am a member of the press and we have the right to get the story. Remember a public person has no right to privacy. They give that up when they run for office. This is Le Ann Bolton signing off, goodnight."

The reporters turned around and left. By then a crowd had gathered when they heard about Sarah and they were mad. They didn't say anything but if looks could kill, well you know.

Getting into their SUV Le Ann said.

"We should get national coverage with that. That will rile the base up. Everyone will be talking about how Mrs. Nichols didn't want to talk.

"Hey, Le Ann, where did that saying come from?"

"What saying, Bill?"

"The one that says famous people have no privacy."

"It comes from us stupid. We, the press, and the paparazzi."

"If the dumb people out there found out that they are citizens of the United States and have the same right not to be hounded. Why we would all lose our jobs. Don't worry, they're not that smart."

The Dinosaurs

She laughed. They didn't waste anytime leaving town.

Riley led Sarah into the shop. Tom came in behind them, Ida had caught up and entered also. Riley was holding Sarah in his arms, she was crying and shaking at the same time. She looked up at Riley.

"Riley, why did she do that, why?"

"I wish I could tell you, there are just evil people on this earth, all we can do is pray for them."

"You are right, Riley, I will pray for her."

That was Sarah, quick to forgive.

"Tom, who was that?" asked Riley.

"That there was the great Le Ann Bolton. She's the hate machine for the far right conservatives. When they want a dog to bark she runs. That women has more meanness, more evil in her. And she calls herself a Christian. Those that back her up only want publicity. As far as I remember that doesn't get you in heaven."

"Thanks Riley for coming." said Sarah.

"Come on Tom, walk me back to my house." said Ida.

They both looked at Riley and Sarah. He was holding her, she had

The Dinosaurs

stopped crying, she was falling asleep in his arms. She was safe again. His head was leaned on the top of hers. He was gently brushing the hair out of her eyes. Ida and Tom quietly closed the door. There was peace back in town. The sun was going down, the birds were chipping for the night. Sarah and Riley were together again.

All was right with the world.

That night in Washington. The Senator was watching the news. On came the story about Sarah. It was on Murdoch station. The Senator loved it. He knew Le Ann would always get a story. And the base would talk about the wife of the candidate running against him. The pious few, God bless them.

CHAPTER EIGHT

But it had backfired on Le Ann and
Murdoch News Corporation. Le Ann's
daily column was dropped by almost all
of the newspapers that she was in. Even
the media had turned against her, she
was no longer the darling of hate.
Murdoch was facing something also.
His stations were on every cable company
roster. He had his own news program,
MNN. Murdoch News Network. But the
people had done something that had
never happened before. They started
dropping the Murdoch stations form their
programming. They deleted the channels.
Millions of them. That wasn't all, they
then called the cable companies and told
them. They were not finished yet. They
then called the sponsors of the Murdoch
Stations. The sponsors called the cable
companies to confirm this. Soon they
were dropping their sponsorship of the
dropped stations. Why pay for commercials if no one was watching.
When that stopped, one by one the
stations went out of business. Murdoch
tried for a while to pay for them with his
billions. But soon, even the ego maniac,
realized it was lost. The power of the

people, it had shocked the world.

In the Senators office. It was now Mid- September and things were too close for Senator Adams. The race was a dead heat. Forty one per cent for Riley and Forty three per cent for the Senator. He had never had a race this tight before. He called in his shock squad. Sitting around the table was Jack, Sam and the Senator.

"Things are just too close, we have to do something." said the Senator.

"We've tried everything" answered Jack.

"Not everything" spoke up Sam.

"What have you in mind, Sam?" asked the Senator.

"It's better you didn't know."

"All I want to know is that you are behind me one hundred per cent." asked Sam.

"Of course I am Sam."

"I will get my boys to head down south, don't worry about a thing." said Sam.

"That's what I like about you, you always come up with something." answered the Senator.

This time they didn't come in a highly visible car. It was an old van with dents and some rust. Inside were Cisco and Padre. They had helped him before, they were Ex-CIA. They owed the Senator some favors, mostly with helping some relatives come over from Mexico. The Senator was always pushing for the immigration bill. He figured that the more that came and the sooner they became Americans the sooner they would vote for him. It was all about the numbers.

Their plan was to get Riley in a compromising position. The Christian Right would go crazy. They went into a bar a found Riley. He had been drinking heavily. Maybe the pressure was getting to him. They knew they had the right man, because everyone was calling him by his name. Riley. They scooted up to the bar, each took a seat on both sides of him. They started small talk.

"How's it going?" asked Padre.

"Busy, Busy" replied Riley.

"All this election business keeping you busy, I bet" said Cisco.

"You never know, putting up all those signs." Riley replied.

"I bet, here have another drink." offered Cisco.

"Thanks," answered Riley

Soon it was time for the bar to close. They offered to take Riley home, after all he was too drunk to drive. They left holding him up Riley between them. The bartender wondered who they were, but Riley always did have some strange friends.

They through him into the van. Inside was Penelope.

They had to drive all the way to Charlotte to find a prostitute. There wasn't even a dog walking the streets at night in Newton.

"Drive to the motel." ordered Padre.

Inside they put Riley with his briefs on next to Penelope. She had on a sexy outfit. She was holding him tight as if she was making five hundred dollars. Oh yea, she was.

They men took several pictures and left.

"Hey, what about me. I got to get back to Charlotte."

Penelope yelled to the men leaving in the van.

"You got paid, find your own way."

Penelope stomped her feet causing the money in her hands to fall. It started blowing all over the lot. It was quite a sight. Penelope running with her outfit on. She passed the night clerks window with her outfit blowing. Inside was Seth. He was about seventy years old. Never married. He was drinking his nightly coffee. When Penelope ran by he dropped his coffee and started coughing. He had never seen anything like that in Newton before. He would never forget this night either.

They gave the photos to Sam and he gave them to what was left of the Murdoch Stations. They went on air the next night. The Senator was pleased, this would sink that Riley's ship for sure. One thing, though.

Back in the bar Riley was sitting at his usual seat.

"How you feeling Riley?" asked the Bartender

"I've felt better, had way to much last night." answered Riley.

"Who were those two guys?" asked the Bartender

"Don't know, never seen them before." answered Riley

The late night news was on from Charlotte. There was a news bulletin flashing across the screen. Breaking News.

"We just got this in from anonymous sources." said the announcer.

"It's pictures taken of Candidate Nichols caught in a hotel with a prostitute."

They showed the pictures.

The Dinosaurs

"Hey, Riley, that's you. Who is she?" asked the bartender.

"Don't know, I don't remember anything after I left here"

One thing though.

"Back at the campaign office Tom and Riley were watching the same news program. What? Another Riley?

"Hey, they got my cousin on there, turn it up." Said this Riley.

"Again this will probably sink the hopes of Riley Nichols running for office." repeated the news anchor.

What Cisco and Padre didn't realize was that Riley was a family name. Several of Great Grandpa's sons and Grandsons were named for him. The one in the bar just happened to be Riley Taylor, first cousin to Riley Nichols. Riley and Tom just broke out laughing, their sides began to hurt.

Back at the bar, Riley Taylor was being patted on the back and trying to answers questions about his fifteen minutes of fame.

"Come Riley who is she, tell us all about it."

"I swear I don't remember anything." Riley tried to tell the truth.

"Sure you don't" The bar erupted into loud laughter.

The Dinosaurs

In Washington, Senator Adams was in his office watching the same program. Sam had called to tell him about the airing. The Senator had Satellite and he tuned into the station. What he saw didn't make him happy.

"Nooo....ooo!" he shouted.

"That isn't him, you got the wrong guy!"

He was throwing the magazines everywhere. Looks like Debbie will be picking them up in the morning.

CHAPTER NINE

The light was flickering off the walls of the room. It wasn't supposed to be there. Off in the distance he could he the sounds of a siren wailing. Something was wrong. He awoke with a start. The light and noise were coming from outside his front window. He got out of bed and looked out the upstairs window. His truck was on fire! Down the road he could see the Fire Department coming at full speed. They didn't know it was only the truck. All they knew was a person was here and he might need help. The Fire Truck skidded to a stop near his truck, the firemen jumped out, got out their hoses and started to cover his truck with water. Several others ran over to the house and kicked open the door and ran in to see if anyone was inside. The chief who was in a car behind the Fire Truck stopped, got out and ran over to the house. The firemen came into Riley's room.

"Riley, come with us, we're checking the rest of the house for fire." shouted the lead fireman. Riley went with them downstairs. Outside he met with the Chief.

"You alright?" the Chief asked Riley.

"Yea, what happened?" Just then a fireman came up to the chief and said,

"Everything's alright in the house, only Riley home, Chief."

"Keep hosing the front, in case this truck decides to explode." cautioned the Chief.

Soon the fire was out. The fireman were rolling up their hoses and putting them back on the truck.

"Thanks, guys." said Riley to the firemen.

"Sorry we couldn't save the Old Grey Ghost, Riley." yelled one back.

"I know you gave it your best."

"Sorry about the door." said another.

"That's alright, under the same circumstances you are welcome to do the same thing." answered Riley.

The fireman smiled at that. The Chief and Riley had moved to the front porch.

"Riley, I'm calling my Arson Investigator, I'm no expert, but if I had my druthers, it looks set."

"No Kidding, Wow, who would do that?" asked Riley.

"That's what we intend to find out Riley."

The Sheriff said while walking up to

them. They hadn't noticed him drive up.

"Riley, you Ok?" asked the Sheriff.

"Yea, never expected this." replied Riley

The Chief of Police of Newton was next to ride in. Even though it wasn't his beat, he also knew Riley.

"Hello, Sheriff."

"Hello Chief" All of them knew Riley.

All of them considered him family. The Chief of Police, the Sheriff and the Fire Chief gathered by themselves in the yard, talked a little while and came back to Riley.

"Look Riley" said the Sheriff.

"We think you need some protection."

"No, don't say anything, I know how you will answer.

"I'm going to leave a deputy here until morning until I can arrange some more, the Chief says he's sure he can get plenty of volunteers from the city department to come.

"No," he said when Riley was going to answer him.

"Riley someone is either trying to scare you or hurt you, and we in Catawba County and Newton will not let it happen to one of our own. End of conversation."

The Sheriff turned around and left.

The Dinosaurs

"Riley, we are going to keep a good check on strangers in the city, too." said the Police Chief as he left.

"Don't touch anything, my man will be here first thing in the morning."

"Try to get some sleep, it's going to be a long day tomorrow.

It was a short night. Riley got up, took a shower, got dressed and went downstairs to get some and started the coffee pot. He was just sitting down at the kitchen table when someone knocked on the front door.

"Man" he said out loud.

While walking to the door he saw it was Tom Peters.

"Come on in Tom, the doors unlocked." he yelled. Tom opened the door and that's when all the noise and ruckus from out side came flooding in.

"Geez."

"Can't those firemen be a little quieter, what are they doing tearing my truck apart?" asked Riley.

"You mean you don't know, haven't you looked outside?"

"Just got out of the shower, was fixing to eat, what's up?"

"Come here, look for yourself." said Tom opening the door for Riley.

"Riley looked out, he was stunned,

the whole road in front of his house were covered with satellite trucks from different television stations in North Carolina and beyond. The reporters were standing behind a make shift line of yellow police 'Do Not Cross tape'. Most were talking on microphones while cameras were taping them. The Sheriffs Dept had to add more deputies during the night as the mobile trucks started pouring in.

"What caused this, Tom"

"Don't you remember that little fire last night?" asked Tom.

"Sure, but all this?"

"It's become world news Riley, about a candidate whose truck was set on fire, possibly even his life threatened.

"I don't think it will go that far?" answered Riley in disbelief.

"It changed this morning, when someone spray painted the water tower."

"Spray painted the water tower?"

"Yea, sometime early this morning, probably when the fire alarm started."

"Someone painted, We Don't Want Indians for Senator."

The Chief of Police and the Sheriff don't believe it's anyone local. It has to be an outsider."

"I agree with that, that doesn't

sound like anyone from Newton or Catawba County." agreed Riley. The reporters spotted him at the door and they all started yelling.

"How do you feel about this attempt on your life, Mr. Nichols?"

"Do you think that Senator Adams is behind it?"

"Let's go in." said Riley.

A dark blue sedan pulled up and through the marked tape line. It stopped when a deputy stepped in front of it.

The deputy had a brief conversation and looked at the drivers wallet that he was holding up. He let the car through. Out came two men dressed in blue suits and blue ties. They stopped in front of them on the porch.

"Mr. Nichols?"

"Yes?" he answered

"This is agent Dodd and I'm agent Gentry, we are from the SBI. (State Bureau of Investigation) The Governor sent us down here to see to your protection."

"My protection?"

"Yes Sir, after what happened last night and the City Water Tower incident, we feel you are in danger and the Governor doesn't want anything happening to you."

The Dinosaurs

"I really don't think...." started Riley.

"Sir, it's best we work together, we are going to follow you anyway." the agent smiled.

Riley got the hint, they had a job to do.

"Alright, what do I do?"

"Let's go in, we're explain how we operate."

"Oh, I'm sorry, by all means come inside, do you want some coffee, I just put some on?" asked Riley.

"That does sound good, Mr. Nichols."

Sitting around the kitchen table the agent was finishing up his briefing.

" Agent Dodd and me will be by your side at all times. We will have additional men assigned too. You will not see them, but we will see you."

"Thanks, guys, I don't know what to say, I never had Secret Service before."

"Sir, we are not Secret Service, but we operate the same, you are our first priority."

"Sorry" responded Riley.

"That's alright, people make that mistake all the time, we don't mind."

So it came to be that Riley had people guarding him. Tom was getting the inside story. His newspaper were being sold out every time they printed a new story. His editor was pleased as punch. But it had become much more than a story to Tom. He had become a friend to Riley. He was pulling for Riley. Wouldn't be something if he did win.

They stopped by Sarah Shop to introduce them to her. She came to the front of the shop.

"Hello Darlings,"

"Come on in, have some of my Lemonade."

"My, those blue suits look good on you."

That was Sarah.

The agents found out it was a hardship protecting Riley. They had only been there a week. All the people in Newton knew about them. When they went with Riley to the stores, restaurants, or even just walking downtown, they found out it was dangerous. All the women came out of the stores and some out of their houses, each offering free bites of cakes and of course coffee, ice tea and a thing called the Newton Special.

The Dinosaurs

The receipt was. 4 ½ to 5 cups
apricot nectar. 1/3 cup Lemon Juice, 2
cups orange juice and ½ cup light
corn syrup. Combine all, chill, serve with
lemon and orange slices.

The agents didn't know what was in
it. All they knew was that it had a kick.
They weren't sure if they were not
breaking the law, they didn't know what
they were drinking, was legal.

Between the agents and the locals
Riley was in good hands.

CHAPTER TEN

"It doesn't seem like it's going to work, Sam" said the Senator.

"It should have scared him off, especially the water tower thing." answered Sam. Jack came into the office, he had the latest polling data.

"How bad is it?" asked the Senator.

"Pretty bad, Pa Pa, it has you at forty per cent and Nichols at fifty five per cent."

"We have to get serious, now, we can't lose everything we have built up here."

"Being a Senator is like building your own company. You start off from scratch, build relationships with other Senators and Corporations, with the government agencies. You start off making nothing, get a raise every year and have money pouring in from those that you did favors for, have a great retirement and medical benefits, he wants to come in and take it away from us."

"We can't let that happen" said the Senator.

"Sam, got anything left?" asked the Senator.

"Sure, but you have to approve it

and back me one hundred per cent if anything goes wrong." replied Sam.

Look Sam, you know I will be behind

"Whatever it is, go for it."

"And hurry, we don't have much time left."

It was early morning, things have settled down since the fire. Riley had a new vehicle to campaign in. It was a bus, not a big as Senator Adams, but it had all the modern conveniences, and it was just big enough for Riley, Tom. Sometimes one of the SBI men would ride along inside. It was parked out behind the Gas Station. Usually Bryan Hughes would give tours to the town children or to town folks who had relatives in town. They had never seen a campaign bus before.

"Where's your next stop, Riley?" asked Dodd. They were all calling him by his first name now.

"I think we got scheduled to go to Ashville, Dunn and on to Elizabeth City." answered Riley looking at a piece of paper.

"Boo....oooom!!" Came a loud explosion that shook the glass in the front of the gas station. The agents Automatically jumped up and covered Riley with their bodies. After a few seconds when nothing else happened they all went outside to see what had caused it.

In fact the people that were down-town that day and the merchants all were standing outside on the sidewalks. Riley say a large billowing smoke coming from the Green Street Area. All in a row, behind each other came the fire trucks, the EMTs and the police. Then came the Chief of Police. He squealed to a halt in front of the gas station.

"Get in Riley, it's Sarah, it was her shop." yelled the Chief.

Riley and agent Dodd jumped in the back seat and they took off. Not far behind was the other agent and Tom. They jumped in the agents car and headed that way. Tom was up front with the agent when he noticed that he was using his phone to call his headquarters.

"Yes that's right, an explosion in Newton, at Mr. Nichols ex-wife's business. Yes, send a explosion expert here fast as possible, don't worry we are watching him, I'm sorry we didn't see this coming."

"Yes, Chief, someone wants Riley out of this race pretty bad."

"And Chief, this just became personal,

The Dinosaurs

I want that Son of a Gravedigger."

"I know Chief, I will calm down, but this lady didn't have a bad bone in her body."

"Ok, Chief, bye." Tom noticed that the agents eyes were wet. This was indeed personal. When they got to the shop the EMTs were carrying Sarah out on a stretcher. She had an oxygen mask on, her face was singed from the blast. She was not conscious.

"She's going to Catawba Valley."

Said one of the EMTs to Riley. She went straight onto the ambulance and on to Hickory. The lights and siren blowing. They had to get her there fast. She didn't look so good. The front of the store was a shambles. The whole front was blasted away. Glass was everywhere. The Police were trying to back up the crowd that was gathering.

"Move back, please, this is a crime scene, please move back." said one officer. Even though the officers had never experienced this type of thing before, they had been well trained, soon the people were moved back, and the scene was secured with crime tape. The detectives were here and the team for the fire department also. A detective came out of the store and came up to Riley.

The Dinosaurs

"Sorry, Riley, I think she was lucky it didn't kill her right away. She must have been looking at something behind the Counter when it exploded. Might have saved her life."

"How is she?" he asked.

"I don't know, they just took her to Catawba Valley." answered Riley.

"Need a ride there?" asked the Chief. A helicopter came in fast and low. It landed in the park across from the store. Out came man dressed in a suit. He walked over to Riley and the agents.

"Holy Cow!, it's the Chief, said Agent Dodd."

"Mr. Nichols?" he asked while extending his hand to shake.

"Yes?"

"I'm Mike Sessions, head of the SBI, I came as soon as agent Dodd called me."

"We are here to help you anyway we can."

"I appreciate that Sir, I just want to get to the hospital and see about my wife." He still called her his wife. Always have, always will.

"Agent Dodd, what have you got on this?"

The Dinosaurs

A Newton City Police Officer walked up to the group of men.

"Excuse me Chief, three men turned toward him, I have some information on that vehicle.

Everyone looked in his direction.

"A van was spotted passing the store about the same time it blew up. It has a dent with green paint on the rear left of the bumper."

"Also have the tag number."

"Great work"

"Wasn't us Chief, it was that kid over there on that bike. Seems like the driver didn't like the kid staring at him, told him so in not so nice way."

The City Police Chief looked at the Detective and said, "Get right on it."

"Right Chief" said the Detective walking toward the makeshift Command Center.

The Chief yelled to the Officer.

"Sandy, give that kid a Lollipop."

The officer stood there for a moment. The kid was at least fifteen years old.

"Ugh, Chief, don't you think he's a little to old?" asked Officer Sandy. The Chief thought for a second.

"Yea, OK."

"Go shake his hand."

The Dinosaurs

"Huh?"

Too late, the Chief had walked away.

Sandy, one who always obeyed orders, went over an shook his hand. The boy just looked at him.

"Mr. Nichols come with us, we will fly you there."

"Thanks" Him and the chief left on the helicopter heading to Hickory.

The helicopter landed next to the Catawba Valley Hospital, the ambulance with Sarah had already arrived. She was in the Emergency Room getting treated. A Hickory Police Officer was guarding the door to the Emergency Room. He held up his hand when Riley and the Chief approached him.

"Officer, I'm Chief Sessions from SBI and this is Mr. Nichols." stated the chief.

Still couldn't pass, they both had to show their ID. Riley stood near the entrance to the room where they were treating Sarah. He watched as the doctors and nurses were working feverishly on her. They were on mission and that was to save her life. They were tubes running in and out of her. Her face was still red from the burns. A nurse was kindly wiping off the dirt and grime off her. Not in a rough way, but gentle but efficient way. You could tell these doctors and nurses were professional in all ways, but they were still human beings and they cared for their patients.

Back in Newton. Most of the townspeople had gone home or to business to discuss what had happened that morning. Some had gone to local churches to pray for Sarah. The agents were still with the local agencies to find out what had happened. All were working as a team. Tom, Harry Bingham, John Harrell, Jim Nixon and Bryan Hughes were at the gas station waiting and praying for Riley and Sarah. In the back ground was the police radio that everyone kept in their house or business.

A voice broke the silence.

"Central this is 104, I have that van spotted on Highway 321 going south toward Maiden."

The whole town came alive, everywhere the townspeople were alert, listening and staring at their radios. It was no different at the gas station.

"104 this is Central, do they see you?"

"They know I'm here they keep looking in the rear view, I haven't put on any lights, I'm waiting for backup."

"Stay with them 104, backup is coming."

The Dinosaurs

Most of the new police radios you can get several police agencies on the same radio. So you could hear one police agency call and another answer.

"Central, Newton, calling Catawba County dispatch"

"Catawba here"

"We have a van involved in the 402 this morning, heading south on 321, can you assist?"

"That's a big 10-4, pardon, affirmative."

"104, this is Central, where's your 10-20?"

"Just passing "J" street, heading south, normal rate of speed."

"10-4"

"County, you copy?"

"10-4" ,

"Have four County units on way."

"Central this is County, units at 155 and 321"

"10-4, County"

"104, you copy"

"10-4"

The word had traveled like wildfire. People were stopping on the sidewalks, even pulling over there vehicles to park and go inside to listen. The town was at a virtual stand still. More people had come into the gas station, it was like listening to game seven of the World Series, in the ninth inning, all tied up. It was as if was play by play announcing.

The radio crackled again.

"Central, 104, approaching 155 at 321"

"10-4"

"You copy County?"

"10-4"

The van saw the County Sheriffs vehicles at all the exits on 321 and the driver panicked. He gunned his van and headed south on 321.

"104, Central, he's gone rabbit, he's on the run."

"104, 10-80"

"10-4"

"County?"

"10-4, in pursuit with city 104"

"Rabbit? What Rabbit? How did a rabbit get in this?" asked Jim Nixon.

You could hear the sirens in the background while they were talking on the radios. The town was going crazy.

"Get um, Go get um!" they shouted.

"104 Central"

"Central,104"

"Be advised to units down the road he in excess of 100 mph."

"10-4"

"Don't lose him 104, go 104!" the

crowd yelled in Hughes Gas Station.

"104, Central he approaching 321 and 150."

"104, Central, he's exiting 321"

Unbeknown to the van driver, local truck divers had been pulling their tractor trailers onto the off ramps and blocked the way off.

"104, he's 10-50 in a ditch."

"Get um 104, get um!" the crowd yelled louder.

" 104, to Central, they've gone rabbit again, they're on foot heading toward the woods. In foot pursuit, on mobile."

"Rabbit? What Rabbit? Will someone please tell me about this rabbit?" asked Jim.

"Central, this is County, we are on foot behind them."

Soon there were truck drivers, Sheriffs Deputies, and 104 in hot pursuit on foot. The people in the area were stopping and looking at all this going on. It looked like the fox hounds had been holed up for a month. Then let out and were rabid with the chase. All you could see was policeman, deputies, trucks drivers, all running in different directions. Chasing three foxes, men, who had no where to go. It was like the

The Dinosaurs

Oklahoma land rush. One was tackled by two deputies. One was gang tackled by some truck drivers. And one was tackled by 104. There was silence for a minute. The whole town was silent, holding their breaths, waiting for the winning field goal, holding their breath until it went through.

"What!" said one citizen holding his arms out as if praying for the radio to speak. Next came a clear calm voice.

"104 Central"

"Central"

"10-95"

"All in custody"

"Central to County.....Thanks"

"County to Central, good luck, God Bless."

All around Catawba County. All around Newton. Every truck stop, every Police and County headquarters in the area. All around you could hear people yelling. They were high fiving each other and jumping around.

"Got them, they got them!!" Yes indeed, they got them.

"Will someone please tell me what happened to that rabbit?" asked Jim.

In the hospital room sat Riley beside the bed where Sarah was sleeping, sleeping, she was in a coma. She still had tubes in her arms and oxygen on her face. Her face was still red from the explosion. She had suffered a severe concussion. She was lucky she was alive. But she wasn't through the woods yet.

The room was sterile and quiet, except the noise of the machines helping Sarah. That constant sound that let you know she was still here. Riley held her hand, he had done his crying earlier. Now, he had made up his mind, he was getting out, it was not worth losing Sarah to be Senator.

The door opened. In walked Agent Dodd.

"Riley, thought you would like to know, they got them." he said in a low voice. Riley looked like the air went out of him.

"Think God, tell the boys I appreciate it with all my life." said Riley.

"They know Riley, they know." with that the agent left the room, shutting the door quietly.

Back at Hughes Station, Tom and the fellows were talking. John Harrell said,

"So he's made up his mind."

"Afraid so." answered Tom.

"Can't blame him." said Bryan.

"We came so close, we could have

beat him."

"When will he make the announcement?" asked Jim.

"Tomorrow, at the hospital parking lot, at ten o'clock."

"Sad, just too sad to think about it."

"We got to think about Sarah." said Tom.

"I meant that, it's so sad that good people like Riley and Sarah always have to pay the price for change. The bad always seem to win. Just sad, so sad." repeated Bryan.

CHAPTER ELEVEN

In Washington, the Senator and his staff, well Jack and Robert and Debbie. The Senator was watching the news that announced the wife of Riley Nichols had been hurt in a suspicious explosion. That he would be having a news conference in Hickory, N.C. at ten o'clock in the morning. The announcer said it was expected he would announce that he is withdrawing from running for Senator. Senator Adams smiled and looked at Jack.

"It's too bad about his wife, but sometimes that happens in politics."

"Like collateral Damage in War."

Debbie got up and went back to her office.

"What's with her?" asked the Senator.

"Haven't the faintest." replied Jack.

"Heard from Sam yet?" he asked Jack.

"No, but that's not unusual."

The phone rang.

"Debbie get that." hollowed the Senator into the next office.

"Where is that girl. Jack get that will you."

Jack went over to the Senators desk

and picked up the phone. He talked a few minutes and then said to the Senator. Pa Pa, it's Raymond. Raymond was the code word for Sam.

"Hello, Raymond, how is it going?"

"You are calling from where?"

"Hang up, I'll get in touch with you."

"Yea, 100 per cent, now hang up!" ordered Senator Adams.

By the look on Papa's face, Jack knew it wasn't good.

"What's wrong?" he ask the Senator.

"Sam and his buddies are in jail."

"He wants us to help him."

"Want me to get some lawyers?"

"Are you crazy? We can't get near him."

"There's nothing to tie us in to them."

"He's on his own."

"Oh well, call the news media tell them I will be having a news conference at ten in the morning in the main lobby."

"Let's go eat, I'm starving." said the Senator

Riley was by Sarah's bed in the chair, still holding her hand. He was nodding off tired from the days events.

"Hello Honey, you look kind of bad" said Sarah.

"I look bad" he laughed and she

laughed with him.

"You alright, Honey?" he asked.

"If you don't count that I lost my store, God knows where my cat is. And I'm laying here all tied up to this bed. Yea, I doing just fine."

She laughed again. That was Sarah. He sat with her that night, she soon fell asleep. She would awake during the night, watching him sleep. He would be there all night, and he would be there in he morning.

All was quiet in Catawba County. It had been a hard day for Newton also. Most were in their homes getting ready for bed. Ida was one of them. Her phone rang.

"Who is calling this time of night?" she wondered.

"Well Hi, Mabel, yes, I think that is a great idea. Be right there." Ida got dressed again and went back out. All around Newton and all around the county, heck, all around North Carolina something was stirring.

It was morning. Riley, had taken a shower, changed clothes that Tom had brought him.

"Sure about this Riley?"

"Sure as I can be."

"Alright, be right beside you."

The Dinosaurs

"I know you will Tom, you've been a good friend, I don't know how to thank you." said Riley.

"Stop that or you will have me balling."

Riley walked over to Sarah's bed, patted her on the shoulder, leaned down and kissed her on the forehead.

"Be back in a minute, Honey." said Riley quietly.

Him and Tom walked out of the room and into the hall.

All the Nurses and Doctors and even some patients were standing in the hall watching him. They all were smiling.

"What's going on?" wondered Riley.

Were they happy he was quitting the race. They were like that all through the hospital. Tom and him went out the front door to speak to the news media. All of a sudden a loud yell and applause went up.

"There he is! There he is!" they shouted.

There were hundreds, no thousands of men, women, girls, boys, and even babies of all races and ages.

Riley stopped in his tracks. Tom grinned from ear to ear. It seems that all through the night, people had called each other and agreed to come down to the hospital, some drove hundreds of miles to the hospital to talk Riley out of quitting. The satellite trucks covered on all sides by the size of the crowd, it seemed that they were still coming.

"Mike" the reported spoke into a microphone back to the news station.

"We are on the air and I have never seen, I mean never seen anything like this in my life."

"I swear the streets were empty an hour ago, then we started hearing a low roaring and it got louder and louder and then "Wham!" they burst onto the streets and in front of the hospital. It's over-whelming."

"Riley! Riley! Riley!" The crowd shouted in unison. Riley walked up to the microphone. He raised his arms, started waving his arms and saying,

"Thank You, Thank You"

No one could hear him. The crowd were drowning him out. Finally the crowd quieted down to a whisper. All were watching him. The reporter whispered into his mike.

"Will Riley Nichols still announce that he is quitting the race, what will he do?" asked the reporter.

Riley cleared his throat, seemed to be a lump there.

"Thank you, Thank you, I have to

announce that I am quitting the race to be with my wife."

"No...ooooo, No.....oooo" the crowd. shouted back. Riley looked the crowd over, he saw a boy about the age that his son was when he died. Strange he was the spitting image of him. He was holding a sign that said,

"Do it for Mom"

He jerked back and rubbed his eyes and looked in the direction of the boy. He was gone. Riley stood there staring long enough without moving or talking that Tom leaned over to him, worried about him and said.

"Riley you alright, what were you looking at?."

"My son, I was looking at my son."

"What!"

"Your wouldn't understand, it's an Indian thing."

Riley turned and smiled at him. He then turned back to face the crowd."

"Correction, I am here to announce that I am still in this race and I am still going to win!" he yelled.

The crowd went crazy.

Back in Sarah's room, she said to herself. "Thanks Stephen" You see Sarah had heard about Riley going to quit the race. She prayed to the Lord for him to send a sign to help Riley make up his mind. He sent the best he had. She pulled the covers up to her chin and went to sleep.

"There you heard it first here. Mr. Nichols is still in the race."

He had to cut short his reporting cause people were jumping up and down with joy all around him.

"They're going crazy here, got to go."

He signed off but the camera's stayed on. Even the Police officers, the firemen, the SBI agents, the Doctors and Nurses and patients that could, were hollowing and jumping with joy. This is one time that Catawba Valley wasn't quiet.

Meanwhile, back in Washington. Senator Adams was standing in the main lobby. He was making a speech on what had happened to Candidate Nichols and his wife. There were only four reporters in front of him.

"What happened to all the reporters, don't they know this is breaking news." asked the Senator.

"First let me tell you how sorry I am for Mr. Nichols and his wife. I dearly hoping that she gets well soon. I am sorry that he felt that he had to drop out of the race but its understandable. It's lucky that the State of North Carolina has such a long standing Senator already here. I will continue to fight for your rights and I will always listen to..."

A reporter rushed up to the other reporters and yelled.

"He's still running!, Riley is still running, there are thousands at the hospital, what a rally cry they are yelling."

"Do it for Sarah, Do it for Sarah."

The other reporters knew where this news story was going, no where. They all ran outside to get in their cars and down to their networks to work the story.

"Poof" they were gone.

Standing there all alone was the Senator and Jack. Their mouths were open.

"Better shut those mouths, flies will get in." said a passing Security Guard.

Riley was spending the next two weeks until the election with Sarah. It took about a week when she came out of the coma. She was still weak. Her face and arms and hands were healing fine. Doc said should be no scarring. It didn't matter to Riley, he would take her scars and all. The Senator seemed to have disappeared. He wasn't doing any news conferences like before. It was oddly quiet, one week before the elections. That was fine with Riley, the more time he could spend with Sarah.

The big night was here. Riley had his Election Results Party at the local theater, The Green Room. It was packed.

Over in Raleigh, at the RBC Center, Senator Adams was having his Victory Party there. It was only half full.

"Where are all the people, Jack" asked the Senator.

"They're coming later, Pa Pa" answered Jack.

It didn't take long for Riley to know who was ahead. He had overwhelming tallies in the counties that were counted so far.

"You believe this?" asked Tom in Riley ear. It was so loud you had to talk in ones ears to hear.

A women walked up to Tom, she handed him a paper bag. She looked at him and said.

"I'm sorry what happened to his wife, I didn't know, I didn't know. This will help." she walked away.

Tom and Riley looked in the bag and then at each other. A note was inside. It read,

"Give this to the SBI, Debbie"

Tom waved Agent Dodd over.

The Dinosaurs

"Some lady came up and gave me this."

"I know I was watching, you know who she is?"

"No"

"That's Senator Adams secretary. At least she was until this afternoon, she quit." said Dodd.

Dodd took the tapes and went to the back where it was quiet to listen to them. A good agent always has a tape recorder near by. It was all over except shooting the donkey that brought you. Riley had won by a landslide, Sixty Per Cent to Thirty Five Per Cent. The crowd was even louder when Riley came back onto the stage to give his victory speech. He really didn't have one. That was no problem for him. He always spoke from the heart.

The crowd was still loud when he started.

"Thank you, thank you for all your support. Through the good times and the bad times."

His voice cracked. He cleared his voice. I only wish that my darling Sarah could be here. I know she gives you all her love and........

The crowd went silent. It was so sudden that it felt like a boom of nothing. It almost hurt your ears. They were all looking to the side entrance of the stage. There stood Sarah. She was holding a walker in front of her. She was walking across the stage in a slow slide step. One foot at a time. The Doctors told her she wouldn't make it. One thing Riley had learned, don't tell Sarah she can't do something. Riley started across the stage toward her. You could see that Sarah was giving every ounce of strength she had to walk. Along the way she was smiling that crazy smile at him. When she was ten feet from Riley she let out that giggle. That did it, Riley ran to her, grabbed her and hugged her. He didn't want to let her go. And from then on they would remain side by side. The crowd was clapping and crying. It was a night North Carolina would not forget.

It was also a night that Senator Adams would not soon forget also. It seemed that Debbie had hidden tape recorders in the Senators office. On it was the conversations with Sam and Jack about the fire and the bombing of the store. The Senator was giving orders plain and clearly. Maybe the Senator should have helped the lowly people. Say Debbie and her son. He had received six years in jail.

The Senator was leaving the stage at

the RBC Center. It had been a bad night. He didn't know but it was going to get worse.

"Wait a minute Senator." said one of three men in the blue suits that were approaching him on his stage.

"I'll see you in the morning, I'm tired, I'm going home."

The men in the blue suits grabbed his arms, one on each side.

"Hey, are you crazy, I'm a U.S. Senator!" shouted Adams.

"You have the right to remain silent, what you say can be used against you in a court of law..."

"What!, you arresting me?"

"Yes Sir, you are being charged with Conspiracy to Commit Murder. You are charged with attempted Murder on Sarah Nichols. You are charged with..."

"You arresting Me!'

Jack was arrested too. They say he was singing like a bird on the way to the jail. Senator Adams was still yelling when getting into the Police Car.

"You arresting me!" he kept repeating.

There was a man who watched the whole thing. He was running the machine that cleaned the RBC Center lot at night. He was one of those lowly

The Dinosaurs

people. It wasn't like ten million years ago, when man and the dinosaurs didn't see each other. This time man got to witness the second extinction of the dinosaurs.